I0785837

# Circus of Hell

# Circus of Hell

**Chuong Van Nguyen**

**Shrubs Publishing**

# Circus of Hell

In school a bunch of students are invited to go on a trip selected and chosen by an unknown strange looking mystery girl wearing all nothing but black clothes looking dark creepy appearance, the teens were chosen by her sending out invitation with free tickets to go on a trip to some circus open to a secret place where nobody knows about it and the location. She just arrived new here to the school on the first day. Nobody from the school knows who this strange girl is or where she came from. Some school kids say she looks like she came from and resembles a horror movie because she's wearing a black dress with white leggings with her creepy long black hair covering her face barely to see. She hand-picked the school students without saying a single word to them, the ones that she landed the invitation cards to the students are all accepted, some of school kids find she is quite disturbing and others sees she's quite awesome looking because of her resemblance from a horror movie.

The mystery scary girl came up to one of the last kids of the school chosen to hand out the last invitation to a bloke name Danny, he was the only one brave enough to ask her what's her name and she said her name was Matilda!

Danny assists on asking her more questions as to where she's from and such on but she no longer wish to further speak and not to say anymore and walks off out away from the school and has not been seen again.

His friend Michael also received a card from her as well. They both open the enveloped and looked at it and read what was inside. The invitation tells them to come to the location and this place called special circus just for the chosen ones such as you!

It shows the date and time to arrive there in the next morning sharp where it is also obviously end of the week where kids are off school and have fun in the weekend.

Michael is wondering why it's called SPECIAL the amusement park, its nothing but just a theme park like the rest that he's been all to, over the years says him.

During the school hours moments later after the whole day the bell finally rang in the afternoon everybody is leaving the school to go home.

Michael and Danny are walking out of the school together and Danny sees a clown standing by the tree with a balloon that resembles a clown from the horror movie (the It) waving at him and does the funny scary laugh which makes him notices him at first.

He turns his head and asks his friend Michael does he see that clown standing at the tree near the parking lot.

Michael said he doesn't see anything.

Danny then turns his head back and saw nothing at all he didn't see no clown anywhere.

His friend Michael said to him he must be delusional and paranoid to be seeing things.

Danny replies back and says to him he must be right! He probably is seeing things. He told him that he is delusional and that the clown he just saw gave him the chills since he was a kid. He had the fear of the clown from the It movie and couldn't sleep properly for years since his childhood.

Michael wonders if his school crush would be coming as well!

What Jessica said Danny!

As soon as Michael asks him, He's school crush Jessica comes and appears to him out of nowhere with her other friend name Jane.

She says hi to him and so as her friend Jane.

He smiles at her in a shy way and said hi to her back.

Moments later both of them Danny and Jessica couldn't decide what to say next and both spitted out saying are you invited to go to the circus tomorrow? They both laugh for a bit and Danny was the first to say yes and then later Jessica, Jane jumped in the conversation and said she is also going as well because she got the invitation but  not that anybody really cares about her, she then laughs in an awkward way!

He said that's great to them both Jess and Jane that they're coming along.

Both girls said goodbye to them both and went home separate ways ready for tomorrow.

Michael asks Danny if he would like to come to his party this late afternoon because it's Friday the end of the week.

He said "sure" why not!

They both said see Ya later and went on their separate ways preparing themselves for the party later on.

Later that evening he went to his home getting dressed up ready for the late-night party at Michael's house.

While Michael's parents are having a party also and a did a sleep over with their other relative's house for the night, he did the party on his mom and dad's house without their parents' knowledge, and not even Danny knows about it either. But he wasn't afraid of his parents and cared for less.

Hours later everybody came to Michael's house. Michael is in the party enjoying having a great time before moments later Danny arrived.

During that evening everybody was having a wonderful time getting drunk and so.


The next morning everybody left the party except for Michael and Danny, they both started to waken up slowly feeling exhausted and gotten a hangover.

Danny then warned Michael that he better clean all the messed inside his house before his parents come back home and lectures him.

Afterwards they were finishing cleaning the entire house and they both cheered and started vomiting on the grass together at the same time. After they finish vomiting Michael was the one who just remembered about the Theme Park that they should supposed to go to and told Danny about it.

They hurry it up for all the sudden and went packed up and left the house. In Just for a split-second Michael's parents came back home and ask him how was he doing on his own.

He kind of rushed his parents and had no time to say much and left. Danny and Michael remembered their school crush Jessica and Jane would be there so they would not try to miss out on anything. Their future wive's they said.


They both almost gotten to the specific point where it was written in the invitation located near at their school so the bus driver can pick them up and all the other students to the carnival.

They both rode their bikes as fast as they can but Danny couldn't keep up with Michael as fast because he's still a bit hung over from last night and just moments later, they have finally arrived at their near high school. They arrived and locked their bikes at the pole. As soon as they have done that, they see Jessica and her friend standing at the bus stop waiting so they started to jog towards them.

Luckily, they came on time because the bus has not arrived yet to pick them up.

Just as soon as he came to her, he said "hi"!

Then suddenly the bus came to the exact moment where he was about to ask Jessica something very important.

It doesn't look like it's a normal bus like a school one that the kids had thought in mind, it was a clown bus long enough like it that was chosen for the teenagers. The teens find the clown bus to look very creepy as usual.

The door of the side of the bus opened for them.

Everybody went on to the bus one by one slowly and the door slam shut very loudly for a bus.

Everybody sat on their seats ready to go off to the carnival.

everyone was quiet at first then for a moment some of the students ask around concerning about the scary mystery girl that handed out the invitation that if she would be going also, so one of the students ask the bus driver which was a clown if she would be coming too but the clown did not say a word.


The student that asks the driver was embarrassed and hurt out of ignorance because the clown driver neglected him and went sat back on his seat.

Everybody felt his pain and stayed quiet.

The bus is now moving forward off and away


While they are on the trip to the carnival Danny is seen sleeping leaning against Jessica because he is still tired from last night due to hung over and so as Michael leaning sleeping against Jane.

Moments later Danny suddenly wakes up in a panic mode and tells Michael and the others that he just has had a nightmare.

Michael then tells him he would be alright, it's just only a dream.

Danny wanted them to know that something doesn't feel right about this going to the carnival.

Everybody in the bus started to laugh because one of the students heard what he said and yelled out to everyone saying that he had a wet dream and then suddenly everybody stops laughing moments later because of the clown driver told everyone to shut up in a deep scary voice.

He usually doesn't speak or say a word but that was the only two words he had said so far.


Michael asks Danny does the driver reminds him of one of the characters that looks like Killa clowns from outer space classic horror movie.

Danny is like yeah sure he does, he's quite actually looks like it too.

He tells him that why they both see familiar faces from horror movies since yesterday and till today.

Even Matilda look likes from a horror movie which they mention before.

They are both wondering why for them it's odd to be seeing something strange like this since Matilda gave the invitation a day ago!

Hours of driving some people complaining why it's taking so long to get to the Carnival. Moments later again everybody from the bus fell asleep until the driver beeps its horn, the sound was so loud that it woke and jump scare everyone.

The clown driver gave a deep creepy voice laughs while he opens the door for them to get out.

Everyone gotten out and the bus drove off without saying a word. Every single person from the school hated that clown driver because of his rude behaviour.

But not that it matters to anyone, everybody was just happy that they are finally there to the amusement park. They are all looking around the Theme Park filled with excitement and surprises. They have never seen anything like this one before. This is the biggest amusement park that they have ever seen or been too.

The other clown attendants that work in this amusement park had closed and locked the front gate while when the bus driver drove off out of there but the school kids didn't take notice about it because they were too busy feeling happy about the place looking around the area.

Everyone from the school was happy about this park but only Danny that doesn't feel right about it. He thinks it feels spooky because of his nap earlier.

His friend Michael told him to relax and forget about it and enjoy his fun time in this theme park.

One of the clown employees speaks on the microphone telling everyone of them to have a (hell) of a good time and beeps his horn from his nose twice and laughs.

This is what we call a super fun circus said one of the students, this is the biggest circus they have ever seen even in from a long distance of the areas.

The way the students say it sounds like it will take days to complete all of the games in exaggeration.

Danny is wondering why the people are from the school only but nobody else is around.

Michael doesn't really care who's not around or not, he just wants to have fun. He calls out to everyone saying to all let's have some fun guys!

So, everybody's going headed to different directions to the games they wanted to play that interest them.

When they were playing the games that they chose, most of them wondering why nearly all the games they play is all super cheap so far compared to the circuses that they had went to where everything they charged is expensive.

But not that it really matters to them, they were much happier because everything was so cheap to play and worth the time to go and do the rides and games.

A pop of soda is only ten cents, said Michael!

Usually, a pop of soda is one dollar each in most regular circuses.

So as the rides and the games only fifty cents each game and rides which is unbelievable.

We could be playing this all night till morning. This isn't no regular theme park said they.

But continuously everybody was doing what they are doing, everybody is happy and enjoying themselves.

Danny and Michael were playing the water gun shooting game at the clown's mouth and while they're at it, Danny had beaten his friend.

Michael claims he had beaten him because he was still hung over from last night but he's not buying it. He then received a prize a large bear doll.

Just as soon he won, Jessica and her best friend Jane came up to him unexpectedly asking him how things are going.

He said everything is good so far and asks Jessica if she would want this bear doll he just had won. She kindly accepts it.


The four is heading to the next game walking together in a bunch talking to each other.

The next stop they're heading to the rollercoaster.

But Danny doesn't want to go on it because he said the ride looks so fast and scary.

The others agree on him and heading to a different game instead.

They're heading to a location called a funhouse. While they were inside there, in the mean time they encounter some wild spooky things in the house.

After they're done with the funhouse, they got out of there and said to each other that it was scary but the most fun place to be in.

They started to feel hungry and went to buy themselves some food to eat.

While they were eating corn dogs, Danny turns around and sees a little midget clown behind him.

He speaks to him, and the little clown asks him to come closer so he could whisper into his ears telling him a little something.

He tells Danny if he wants to know in a little secret.

What's the secret he says, and the midget clown tells him, when it gets dark the real fun begins, and then he throws a smoke ball and disappears without a trace.

All three of the others walked up to him asking him what was that all about and who was that little guy that he was talking to.

It was nothing major to worry about he says, and all the midget clown said was when it gets dark there would be more fun like real excitement.

Oh, is that they said Jessica!

So, they moved on playing varieties of the other games and hours later the skies become dark and went pass evening.

Then suddenly a scary siren started coming from the top towers of the speakers of the amusement park.

Everybody from the theme park stood there quietly in a frightening way wondering what that siren is all about.

Everybody seemed confused don't know what's it for.

Seconds later the siren stopped, everybody notices everything from the theme park paused that nothing is moving like someone press the pause button from the remote control.

The lights all went off as well and nobody could see anything clearly, everything is dark and everybody is freaking out until one of the other students took out a cigarette lighter and gave some light.

He was one of the naughty students who smokes and always gets into trouble a lot by the principal.

He asks everybody to be quiet and tells everybody to gather up together to see if everyone was alright.

Until just for a moment he sees something behind Michael and Danny and tells them to look!

They both turn around and saw nothing behind them. They said pothead student guy claiming he saw something behind them that he is high on drugs that he must be seeing things.

Never mind then, he said.

Suddenly the lights went back all on again and everything is moving and working.

But they notice something weird is going on, they notice that all the clowns attendants are all gone from the park without a single trace of any of them at any game sections.

The girls Jessica and Jane is starting to freak out saying that something does not feel so right about this place and that's what Danny had in mind earlier about it too but none of them cared much but they only cared about having fun.

Danny is also scared like the rest and doesn't know what is going on but tries to calm the both girls down anyways.

He convinces everybody to stay calm and get out of this theme park as soon as possible because everybody thinks something is not right so they all go and run for it at the first gate entrance where they came from earlier by the bus.

As soon as they almost had gotten there panicking, they see someone standing at the gate locked in loads of chains impossible for anybody to get out or even escape.

They see an old fancy clown standing there holding up a cardboard.

Jessica yelled out at the clown man asking him can he help them and the clown said nothing back but giggle in his clown voice and it turns out to be nothing but a man size clown doll holding up a cardboard.

Jessica was the one that recognised that it was a man doll and not an actual human because she saw it carefully closer by.

She walks towards it to check it out and so as everybody brave enough to come with her.

She takes the cardboard away out of the clown doll hands to see what it says on it.

What does it say, Danny asks?

It says, what everyone's scariest horror movie icon is since their childhood.


For a moment everybody is thinking inside their minds about what are their scary horror icons until Jessica flips the cardboard backwards.

She said wait a minute there is more, it says from the back!

Again, Danny asks her what does it say?

It says congratulations, you will now meet your scary icons starting from now before they seek in ten seconds flipping from this card box.

The countdown begins.

She drops the cardboard from her hand with scare in vain, she doesn't know what she is going to do next.

Tears are running around her eyes believing that all this must be real.

Danny tells everybody to go run and find a hiding spot. He quickly grabs her hand running to find a place for them to hide as well.

Everybody has found a hiding spot already and the ten second countdown is over. Moments later people were complaining they don't see nothing happening.

Then out of nowhere, there were strange sounds coming from around the gaming sections.

They can hear a loud scratching screech sound from a metal pole in a distance. They can hear someone's familiar laugh.

Don't tell me what I think it is, said Michael!

They said they can see someone lurking from the shadows popping out which looks like to be a human figure with a scissor's claws on his right arm.

Michael looks closer to see who he thinks it is and he was spooked out.

He quietly whispers to the others saying that it's him, it's Freddy Krueger. He is one of my main horror icons.

Everyone can hear him laughing.

Then another sound came from another spot, a gurgle sound and Jessica knows who that sound is, she said it's Kayako Saeki from the grudge movie! That's her main horror icon that scared her since she was a child.

And then chucky from the child's play movie appeared with the same goes as Pennywise the clown from the It.

Both horror icons belong to Danny and Jane.

There were more that came out of that  belong to the other students.

Everybody started screaming and running away from their nightmares while Freddy said he can sense and smell Michael's fear from a distance hiding away somewhere.

You can run but you can't hide to him said Freddy.

He is now afraid and couldn't move from the spot while Jane tried to grabbed his hand forcing him to run away with her until chucky appeared out of nowhere and gave her a scary Peek a boo!


They both screamed in fear but luckily were able to get away.

Everybody was running away screaming where ever they could get away from their scary icons because they're being chased by them.

Everyone was running for a moment until the four meet up with each other again.

Danny told the three to follow his lead to get to one of the mini houses.

When they have gotten into the different mini fun houses, they try to lock the door by using a sledge hammer.

While they were doing that, they didn't take notice what was behind them when they got into the house.

There was a chubby man tied to a chair dressed in clown clothes with his mouth covered in socks.

None of them knew what to do. They didn't know what to expect and do next, but he scared them at first.

They don't know whether they should untie the man or just leave him there.

Jessica was the one first that responded and untied him.

After that the clown man thank her and was about to leave when she asks him for help. She assumes he must be a good clown that was tied on to a chair and tortured by the evil ones.

The chubby clown man said he could help them since they helped him.

So then, he told the four to follow him all the way to the back outside of the backyard where there is a toilet.


The toilet is unusable.

The toilet room from the outside backyard has a secret tunnel that could lead them to an exit at some place.

The man showed the four and led the way and it took forever and ever for them to exit the tunnel.

When they finally reach outside from long crawling in the tunnel, all five were tippy toeing to one of the game sections hiding behind it making sure no one is noticing them.

They all witness something from their very eyes which is out of this world.

They see the rest of the other students being tortured and dragged down to hell by their horror icons. They're pulled down into the earth's portal from hell.

They can hear the students from their school screaming and crying for help but nobody is there to help any of them.

The chubby clown man explains to the four that once they have taken the students down to hell, those horror icons from the movies that they imagine with fear are all gone as well and cannot be touched or harm other kids, and that is the rule of this game.

Nearly the rest of the other students are all taken down to hell while there are still left such as Danny, Michael, Jessica, Jane and a few others.

Danny mentions to the chubby clown man can they be killed to avoid going to hell and he also asks why are they going to hell and what have they done to deserve such a thing?

Yes, they can be killed and avoided hell.

But he does not know himself the reason why the school kids such as them four and the others are going down there.

He says if they are brave enough to kill them, then they will be set free!

When the chubby clown man explains to them, Danny came up with some sort of strategy.

He tells the group just like in the movies they all have to work together in a team in order to survive and win. This game can be beaten, says him.

And so, they did, everybody listen to him and follow his idea.

Danny mentions something like a trap in order to beat this.

There are lots of electricity and cables in this theme Park, he said he could use them as a weapon to eradicate their childhood nightmares once and for all.

Danny explains and tells Jane she can kill Chucky like nothing because he's just a size of an infant doll which he says he could be killed easily just like in most of his movies. He asks her to go find another sledge hammer and beat the living crap out of him, splatter him, he said.

And as to Jessica, she has to continue being brave and keep decoying Kayako Saeki by running around anywhere just to buy them some time to create a trap.

And as for him and Michael's childhood horror icons Pennywise and Freddy Krueger, he tells Michael to make them fight each other by confusing them, to make them fight each other is to make them hate each other that simple.

They all went and did what Danny had planned out.

While they were doing that, moments later Michael yells to Danny to hurry it up with his trap.

Michael is busy stalling the two for him when Jane and Jessica are busy with the others.

Chucky died moments later by the sledge hammer from Jane, Jessica is still on the run being brave from Kayako Saeki and Michael is continuously making fun of the two Pennywise and Freddy Krueger.

They both couldn't handle his jokes and lies anymore about them and started to fight each other with anger.

Michael was at stared point and was laughing by covering his mouth because the plan that Danny said actually worked.

After that Danny had finished up with his trap.

When he had finished with his trap, Pennywise had killed off Freddy Krueger and for the count only comes down to two the It clown and Kayako Saeki.

Danny shouts out the three to come all together to trick the remaining two.

When they have gotten together Jessica said Kayako was a hard ghost to kill. She said she tried many traps herself to eliminate her but she couldn't, she always comes back.

This time Danny said this fifty/fifty chance it might work his plan to trap and eliminate them.

The four lured the two of them by taunting them to come closer and the wires got tangle to their feet, Danny quickly runs to the power circuit and turns the switch into high voltage and electrocuted them both. He turns it even to a much higher volt which meets to its maximum peak.

Both the Pennywise and Kayako Saeki body was exploded with full electricity and was eliminated from the game.

The four cheered for victory and the chubby clown man smiled at them.

It is now over, they said.

They were looking around to see if anybody from their school was still here besides them and unfortunately there was nobody left but only them.

This time they all ran to the front gate where they came from during the afternoon to exit the theme park to see if the gate has been re-open.

They assume that it must be open because they have ended the game by eliminating their horror icons.

The gate was still shut with loads of chains covering it.

They were disappointed but Michael said he can try to climb over the top of it and when he does, he got repelled and bounce backwards and fell to the ground.

The area must have some magnetic field surrounded the place where nobody could escape from this place.

They ask the chubby clown man is there another way to get out of this place and he said there might be another way to get out, so he told the four to follow him.

They followed him all the way to a circus show room that they have not been to as yet it looks like a total abandoned.

He said inside this show case can lead them to the exit of this amusement park. They have to go all the way on top of the raft to do the death dive down into the swimming pool for them to escape this terror park.

They wanted to ask him more questions because the way he describes to them doesn't make sense which sounds really odd to them on how something like this could lead them to exit but he just hurries them to go up.

So, they trusted him with their instincts and went to the top and when they finally reach there, they did not see him the chubby clown man anywhere from the bottom.

Where did he go, says them!

They were calling for him the clown man but he was nowhere to be seen.

All four kept walking to the tip of the edge and suddenly see the pool water changed and turned into lava swirling around making it into a portal to see through gates of hell.

It was a door to hell not an exit to the theme park.

They now know the chubby clown man was deceiving them this whole time and that he is a part of this game.

When they were all staring down at the pool of hell, they can hear a gurgling sound behind them.

They turned around and saw Kayako Saeki.

Jane couldn't take it anymore and she was way too afraid compare to the rest, she literally jumps off the raft down into the depths of hell.

Michael yells out, no!

The grudge ghost girl is getting a bit closer to them until Jessica and Danny sees Michael crying and jumped into the gates of hell with her.

Kayako is getting really close to them now.

Danny yells to the ghost, aren't you suppose to be dead already.

You just won't die would Ya said he!

As soon as he said that, Kayako Saeki pauses for a moment. Her entire body turns and twitches very fast and changed to somebody else.

They were surprise to see who it is, it was Matila

Matilda handing out free tickets had disguised herself as Kayako Saeki's image.

She said to them that they have already killed Kayako in this mind game, she said she is not her. She is Matilda!

Besides that, Danny yells to Matilda in a trembling voice what does she want from them and who is she?

He also asked her why everyone she picked from their school are all going to hell.


Before she tells them the reason of these all, she wanted them two to know, do they know they're already dead.

Danny and Jessica didn't know and looked to be confused.

Before they have gotten here to this amusement park, everybody in the bus is all dead, everyone died from gas that was inside the bus.

Matilda asks them both do they remember the part where everyone was asleep? That was the time where it occurred!

So that's what happened said him!

We were too fatigue to even look back at ourselves without noticing it when we got out of the bus.


She explains to them that she is not a real woman, she is a transgender!

She was the first and only the one from the school that was a transgender back in the sixties.

Danny remembered for a sec that no wonder why everything from this amusement park is all so cheap the fun, fairs and the food.

She continues asking him does he know the actual reason why they were all chosen to come here in the first place.

Matilda asks him can he tell and notice that she is already dead and that she is a spirit.

The whole purpose why they're here for is because of their parents.

The kids that were chosen here were because of their parents that were murderers back in her time.

She further explains to him that she got bullied to the point where she died.

She was on top of the raft here where they're both are standing right now she was pushed by their parents, their parents were pretending to be her friend at the time being, and same goes to the rest of the others.

There was no water down in the pool because the haters made a hole to it and all the water leaked out fast.

She said she got pushed down and died.

It was both your parents who pushed me down, says she!

Now this is going to be their children's that will be pushed down to hell and suffer for eternity. Every one of them should feel my wrath!


Jessica interrupts and wanting to make her some sort of a deal to avoid going to hell because she was about to push both of them down.

She wants to make a negotiation to Matilda.

If her parents did kill her because she was a transgender woman,she wanted to know if they would kill their own mom and dad to revenge her death, would they be free and would not be going to hell.


She said to her that she is a human being and was treated like an animal just for being a trans then their parents should go to hell themselves the way they mistreated her.

Matilda wasn't sure if the two are turning against their words, so she told the two to come to her and touch her hand and show a vision to as what actually really happened, she wanted to make things clearer better than describing to them.

They both now understood the cause of her death, the scene was intensifying and outrage. They made a promise to avenge her, but only in one condition to be able to avoid going to hell. They will not only kill their own parents but to kill the rest of the other student's parents as well in order to avoid everything.

So, they both agreed. The two thinks it's unfair.

Matilda tells them if they don't do it in three days then the deal is off. She then vanishes away in that very spot and waited until the time comes.

Moments later they went back down going to the front gate, they see it finally opens.

The bus that drove them earlier is also at the front gate outside of the amusement park waiting for them.

Danny and Jessica went inside the bus and handed out the rest of the school students IDs by the clown bus driver and the two got back into their bodies and woke up.

Hours later the two have gotten back home and met with their parents looking exhausted.

The two from their sides ask them a question if they know who a young women name Matilda is?

Their parents denied it at first saying they don't know who that person is.

The both sides got furious because they knew their parents were lying.

They were yelling at them to speak out the truth and so they finally did, and confessed.

They ask them is it true that they murdered her back in their time when they were teenagers in school back in the nineteen sixties at the amusement park.

They said it's true, and that she deserved it because everybody looked at her as not a human being. She was a disgraced to human nature and God.

A lot of us are Christians their parents said.

From half Danny's side and Jessica's side they were so hurt to as why they did that to her because they saw the vision that Matilda showed them and they both knew it was wrong in their parents' time and same goes to the rest of the other ones that hurt her.

They went to the kitchen and took out a knife and went to  stabbed them both and told their parents that what they did and explained to them that it was not right. Danny and Jessica stabbed them at their houses and said she is a human being like all of us. Then they continuously stab them to death.

After that, Danny calls Jessica through their telephone landline numbers to meet up with each other for the next following day.

The next day they went on a killing spree of the other student's parents that bullied Matilda to death.

Once they had finally killed every single one of them that Matilda had chosen, they went back to the amusement park to see and meet her once again.

Danny was the one calling for her but she didn't appear straight away, she appeares seconds later. She appears behind them.

She said thanks to them both for doing this for her and that she is now set free. The two will no longer go to hell.

Her spirit and body fades away and she gives them a last good smile in a thankful way.


Everything is now accomplished Danny said, RIP said Jessica. The two hugged each other. And for that very peaceful moment Danny looked at the side and what surprised him that he was not so happy at all.

He sees a bunch of people standing at the front gate which looks to be the siblings of the school students' parents that they had killed yesterday, and they're!

They made a mistake by not eliminating the siblings and now they are just too many of them to stop.

The siblings found out it was Danny and Jessica that mass murdered nearly their entire family.

They saw and catch them on surveillance camera.


The siblings of the parents they killed looked very upset and charged the two.

Danny and Jessica holding each other in fear and said to themselves that this is the end of us, it is not fair at all they say. They set Matilda free while they end up dead for her.

Then the siren started wailing around the amusement park.

Everybody stood still for a second, the people's siblings didn't know what that siren was for and then suddenly it stopped.

They then looked back at the two with rage and saw something behind them.

They saw a bunch of clowns gather in a group holding weapons exactly like they're holding, knives and baseball bats.

Danny and Jessica were confused and shocked to see the chubby clown man there, they don't know whether he is going to lead and kill the both or helping them or help the siblings.

They were confused until both parties charged all together at both sides.

It turns out the clown's side were the onesq protecting the two, but not going against them.

Both sides were fighting together while the chubby clown man grabbed the two and took them out to a much safer place to stand and hide.

They thanked him for the help because they had thought he was against them because he left them at the abandon circus show room.


Jessica asks what his name is because he has never told his name from the beginning.

He said thanks for asking and he said his name is Choppa chop.

The two laughs because it sounds like a candy lolly pop.

The two thanked him again for saving them out there brawling, he said thanks but don't mention it.

Choppa chop thanked them for saving his daughter, for setting her free!

They couldn't believe for a moment that Matilda was  his trans daughter!

Everything seems really confusing to them as to why he was tied to a chair from the start and help them, then disappeared out of nowhere and now reappeared again and helping them.

He said he didn't help them; he was supposed to set them into a trap but had a change of heart because he heard what the two had said to his daughter about helping her eliminate all her killers.

It was the only way to set his daughter free.

And he was proud that they did and now he returns the favour back to them.

He explains further to them both saying that he is a ghost like his daughter and he was about to be set free by the devil from hell because the two had accomplished everything for him and his daughter Matilda.

Choppa chop knew there was something suspicious going on when the two only killed the parent's murderers but haven't killed the siblings.

So, he told the devil he would help them out Danny and Jessica one more time before the deal is now over and he is set free with his daughter Matilda.

The devils want all their souls in order to set the others free he says.

Matilda is now reborn as a real girl this time and Choppa Chop is now reborn as her farther again.

He explains everything to them both and said a final good bye.

Then moments later after he vanishes away, Michael and Jane reappear again out of the sudden.

The four were all happy to have seen each other and hugged in happiness.

Danny wanted to tell the two Michael and Jane about their parents but they said it's ok they already knew the whole thing while they were in hell. They said they were watching them the whole time so there is nothing to worry about. The two agreed to what they were doing.

The four walk out of the amusement park and went somewhere unknown.

THE END